MUM
MONSTER

Read more by Madhurima Vidyarthi

My Grandmother's Masterpiece

Read more for middle-grade readers from Duckbill

Ninja Nani and the Bumbling Burglars by Lavanya Karthik
Ninja Nani and the Mad Mummy Mix-up by Lavanya Karthik
Ninja Nani and the Zapped Zombie Kids by Lavanya Karthik
Ninja Nani and the Freaky Food Festival by Lavanya Karthik
Against All Odds by Ramendra Kumar
Oops the Mighty Gurgle by RamG Vallath
The Deadly Royal Recipe by Ranjit Lal
Vanamala and the Cephalopod by Shalini Srinivasan
Flat-track Bullies by Balaji Venkataramanan
Pops by Balaji Venkataramanan
Ravana Refuses to Die by Rustom Dadachanji
Dhanak by Anushka Ravishankar and Nagesh Kukunoor
Simply Nanju by Zainab Sulaiman
Hot Chocolate Is Thicker than Blood by Rupa Gulab
The Sherlock Holmes Connection by Martin Widmark,
Anushka Ravishankar, Katarina Genar and Bikram Ghosh
Tiger Boy by Mitali Perkins
Karma Fights a Monster by Evan Purcell
Karma Meets a Zombie by Evan Purcell
Karma vs the Evil Twin by Evan Purcell
The Hill School Girls: Alone by A. Coven
The Hill School Girls: Secrets by A. Coven
The Hill School Girls: Strangers by A. Coven
The Hill School Girls: Trouble by A. Coven
The Piano by Nandita Basu
Rain Must Fall by Nandita Basu
Bim and the Town of Falling Fruit by Arjun Talwar
Vanamala and the Cephalopod by Shalini Srinivasan
When Blackbirds Fly by Hannah Lalhlanpuii
Gopal's Gully by Zarin Virji
Ramanujan by Arundhati Venkatesh

MUNNI MONSTER

Madhurima Vidyarthi

Illustrations by Tanvi Bhat

duckbill

An imprint of Penguin Random House

DUCKBILL BOOKS

USA | Canada | UK | Ireland | Australia
New Zealand | India | South Africa | China

Duckbill Books is part of the Penguin Random House group of companies
whose addresses can be found at global.penguinrandomhouse.com

Published by Penguin Random House India Pvt. Ltd
4th Floor, Capital Tower 1, MG Road,
Gurugram 122 002, Haryana, India

Penguin
Random House
India

First published in Duckbill Books by
Penguin Random House India 2023

ISBN 9780143459910

Typeset in Futura Lt BT by DiTech Publishing Services Pvt. Ltd
Printed at Replika Press Pvt. Ltd, India

www.penguin.co.in

Chapter 1

Mishti was almost ten-and-a-half when Munni Monster came to live in her house.

Strictly speaking—as grown-ups often said—Mishti didn't live in a house. She lived in a flat. It was not a laaaarge flat. A medium-sized tight-fit flat with two bedrooms and a kitchen and a big space in between which was dining space and drawing room rolled into one.

This was the space Mishti liked best because it was the largest and no one said anything if she played there or messed about. She could wind her way around the heavy sofas, spread out all her puzzles on the floor, hide under the dining table and pretend it was a cave. No one said, 'Go away, Mishti!' or 'Not here, Mishti' or got cross when they fell over Buboon, the plastic clown.

Not that there were a lot of people to get cross at Mishti. Thamma never ever got cross, which left only

Ma and Baba. And even then, Thamma would jump in and say, 'Aachha, aachha. Never mind, never mind—' and Ma would make exasperated noises and go away.

Mishti loved Thamma best. She loved her stories, her soft snuggly feel when she cuddled up at night. And the papery, wrinkled skin that looked as if it might crack under her fingers. But best of all, she loved Thamma's smell. Her very own special Thamma smell made up of clean and sweet things like soap and Thamma's special perfume.

'Chanel No. 5,' had said Thamma when Mishti first asked her if the smell had a name. 'It's my favourite,' she had said and sighed.

'But why does she use perfume at home?' Riya had frowned. Riya was Mishti's best friend and knew all about everything. 'My mother uses perfume only when she goes out—all very expensive ones, of course—'

'But I don't go out much,' Thamma had smiled when Mishti told her what Riya had said. 'So why can't I use it at home?'

That confused Mishti. She usually believed everything Riya said, but then Thamma didn't sound wrong, did she? So, the next time Riya asked, 'Hey, is your thamma still using Chanel at home?', she pretended not to hear.

On Mishti's last birthday, Thamma had even dabbed two drops of Chanel No. 5 on her wrist. Ooooooh, the smell! She had made the scent last five whole days—

2

the smell on her wrist—simply by not washing that part. She had slept with that hand under her cheek and the gorgeous scent had given her the most beautiful dreams.

'When I grow up,' she had whispered to Buboon, 'I'll have a whole bottle to myself. Or I'll take Thamma's—she keeps saying everything of hers is mine.'

But not all grown-ups were so nice or understanding.

'Poor Mishti,' Tinu mashi had said once, patting her on the head in the irritating way only adults have. 'Poor Mishti, all alone and no one to play with. She really needs a sibling, no?' and she had smirked at Ma in a superior kind of way that annoyed Mishti even more.

Ma was not fazed at all. She was never fazed.

'I don't think we can afford another child, Tinu, or manage another one, to be honest, if she is anything like Mishti. And certainly not in a two-room flat!'

Mishti, herself, had no problems with the two-room flat. Unlike the grown-ups, she owned a little bit of every room. The boring stuff—school clothes, party frocks, that sort of thing—were on a shelf in Ma's almirah, while her desk and books were in the living room. Everything else was in Thamma's room, including the rest of her clothes and all her really important things—Buboon, her toys, her collection of shells and many other wonderful secret things that Ma knew nothing about. And the bed, of course—the old high four-poster bed with its twisty wooden rods and the triangular headboard with its holes and carvings. That was in

Thamma's room too. It used to be Thamma's bed, made especially when she had married Dadu. That had been many, many years ago—many hundreds of years ago, Mishti always thought. But now, Thamma had given it to Mishti.

'I have my own big teak-wood bed,' Mishti would tell everyone proudly. 'Burma teak—the wood came all the way from Rangoon. It's all mine—'

And certainly, the bed was something to be proud of. It stood square in the middle of Thamma's room; as grand as an emperor's throne. Even after so many years, the wood gleamed dark and gold, and the dust in the patterns bristled with pride. A beautiful carved border ran all around the rectangular frame that held the mattress in place, strong and firm even after so many years.

When Mishti had been younger—and shorter—she had to be lifted up on to the bed. Even now it was a scramble, but she could hook her fingers into the carvings and pull herself up, sneezing when the dust flew out.

One day, when Mishti complained about the dust, Thamma had become sad. 'I used to be able to dust it myself. Polished wood looks terrible if you allow dust to settle on it. But my fingers can't manage it any more—look!' And she had wiggled her fingers in Mishti's face. Still beautiful, but wrinkled and all crooked. 'Granny can't manage these nooks and crannies,' she had sung with a funny face. But the tune had been sad.

4

Mishti had hugged Thamma on the spot. 'I'll dust it for you, Thamma,' she had offered bravely. 'Every day, every, every, every day—'

Ma had snorted. Everyone knew Mishti hated dusting. Or cleaning up. Or tidying up of any kind. Every day Ma shouted about toys that had not been picked up. Again. And every day, Thamma picked them up on the sly and put them away. So Ma had reason to snort.

'I *will!*' Mishti had said loudly, when Ma snorted for the second time. 'I will—I will—I—'

'If you do,' Thamma had interrupted them both, 'you can have the bed for your very own.'

That had been two years ago. To everyone's surprise, Mishti had stuck to the bargain. Every single day, she dusted the bed, swirling her duster around the spiral rods and running her slim fingers around the carvings.

Thamma had watched her every day for a whole week before announcing, 'Well done, Mishti! The bed is all yours now!'

And ever since, Thamma had told everyone, 'I sleep in Mishti's bed!'

But Munni Monster was about to change all that.

Chapter 2

Mishti came home from school one afternoon to find Thamma in tears.

That really scared her. Thamma was the happiest person Mishti had ever seen. She never cried, never quarrelled, never got cross. Not even when she was in pain. She had what Ma called 'osteoarthritis', which meant that her arms and legs didn't work as well as they used to. And were all twisted and painful. But even when her knees hurt really badly, she never cried, never complained. So why was she huddled up on the sofa sobbing as if her heart would break?

'Thamma!'

Thamma didn't look up. Ma, who had one arm around Thamma, only shook her head at Mishti and shooed her away with the other one.

It was Baba who explained when he got home a little later. 'Rani di died yesterday, her neighbours called this morning,' he said, his voice all choked up, 'and poor Munni has been left all alone.'

Rani di was Thamma's cousin, her mother's sister's daughter. She lived in a little flat in a very small town about three hours by car. Mishti had met Rani di only once in her whole life while still a baby, so she didn't remember her at all. But Thamma—who had no sister, only three younger brothers—visited Rani di very often; staying for weeks at a time, till Mishti rang up angrily, demanding that she return.

'What fun we used to have!' Thamma was wiping her eyes with the edge of her sari. Her hands were trembling. 'And now—poor Munni is all alone—I must go to her at once.'

'You must do nothing till you've pulled yourself together,' said Ma firmly, her arm still around Thamma.

'But—'

'No buts, we all know what must be done, but we'll do it better if we calm down.'

It was her 'Do-your-homework-no-excuses' voice and Mishti sucked in her breath. Ma never spoke to Thamma like that. But it worked. Thamma blew her nose, nodded and sat up a little straighter.

Very early the following morning, Thamma and Baba left for Rani di's house. Mishti went to school as usual. Thamma had still not returned when she came home, but it was nice to have Ma all to herself for once.

Baba rang Ma before dinner while they were watching *Doctor Mike's Universe* and they were on the phone for a long, long time. And though Mishti was now nearly ten-and-a-half, Ma went into the other room, so she couldn't hear a word of what was being said. Only 'Hmm-hmm, of course. Na-na, no question' and 'No problem at all'.

'Aren't they coming back?' Mishti asked when Ma hung up at last.

'Not tonight—let's eat.' Ma looked at the clock. 'It's getting late—'

'But when are they—'

But Ma was already at the table, so Mishti followed. Ma wouldn't tell her any more just then, she knew.

It was only after dinner, after everything had been cleared away and Mishti had wiped the table down as she did every night that Ma explained.

'Thamma and Baba are staying there for the next few days, because there are many things to decide and arrange. Baba said they should be home by Tuesday—' She stopped as if she wasn't sure of what to say next.

'That's okay.' Mishti came to stand next to her mother. 'That's only three days away—'

'Yes . . .' Again she stopped.

'When they come home,' Ma started again slowly, 'when Thamma and Baba come home, Munni will come with them. Munni, Rani di's sister. She's coming to live with us.'

Mishti looked at Ma, frowning. Munni was—

9

'*Who* is coming to stay with us?' she asked, just to be sure.

'Munni,' said Ma, still in that odd slow manner. 'Munni, Rani di's sister, is coming. Not to stay—to *live* with us. With us, in our flat.'

'Live in our flat? Like, forever?'

'Like forever.' Ma nodded. 'Why? She has her own house and she's an adult—of age—' Mishti was proud of that phrase. She had learnt it from Riya last week. It was so much more grown-up than 'grown-up'.

'Of age,' Mishti repeated, hands on her hips, 'not underage any more—so why is she coming here?'

In reply, Ma gave her that 'duh' look over her glasses. It could mean anything—'You're not *that* stupid, Mishti!' or 'Don't be *stupid*, Mishti!' or 'Now you're being *really* stupid, Mishti!'

Then because Mishti still didn't understand, Ma pulled her close. 'Munni needs a lot of looking after, baby,' she said. 'More than other people her age. She's—she's still like a child in a lot of ways, so—'

'How?'

Ma smoothed away the unruly hair from Mishti's forehead. 'I don't know a lot about her myself—I've met her only two or three times; but from what Thamma says, I know she needs help with her food—'

'Like a baby?'

10

'A little; and sometimes with going to the toilet and—'

'Where is she going to sleep?'

It was the question that had been going round and round in her mind from the moment Ma had told her about Munni. Coiling and uncoiling and hissing at her like a snake waiting to strike.

Ma was rubbing at an old stain on the table.

'Ma?'

'The only possible room is Thamma's, Mishti.' Ma looked her squarely in the face. 'You know that.'

That night Mishti couldn't sleep. Even when Ma had run out of stories and irritably said, 'It's nearly midnight, Mishti, do go to sleep!' She had shut her eyes obediently and turned over. Ma fell asleep immediately, but Mishti couldn't.

'Why can't she sleep in your room?' Mishti asked at breakfast. It was the first time she had opened her mouth all morning.

Ma didn't pretend to misunderstand. She put an extra thick layer of jam on Mishti's toast and said, 'You know she can't. She's not used to us—it would be embarrassing for her—'

'But babies don't get embarrassed,' Mishti pointed out. 'You said she was like a baby—'

Ma fiddled with her cup of tea. 'She's a strange mixture of old woman and little child. Intelligent,

11

sometimes, in the most unexpected ways. Sweet, really—'

'Sweet?'

'Listen, Mishti, I know it's a big change for you—for all of us. But, really, there's nothing else we could have done. She really, truly, has no one else to look after her. And I'm sorry we'll be so cramped in this flat, but there isn't anywhere else we can go—'

'Why can't she sleep on the sofa?' asked Mishti through a mouthful of toast.

'Because—' Ma rolled her eyes. 'You *know* why, Mishti—she needs a room! *Everyone* needs a room! And it's just easier to have you move in with us and for Munni to be in Thamma's room. She needs a proper room and a proper bed and a proper bathroom like all the rest of us. Like every human being ought decently to have!' Ma was getting angry now. 'You should feel sorry for her—the poor thing can't even walk—she has to crawl from one room to the other! And she's just lost her sister, the person who loved her the most and cared for her and did everything for her. The least we can do is to make her feel welcome in our home!'

Mishti left the table without another word. She was angry too, angry inside; about this unknown person who was being suddenly forced into her perfect life. That she would have to give up her room—her bed!—and share Thamma with this-this-

12

'Weird person!' she hissed, as she washed her hands. 'Weird-weird!'

But she said it under her breath, afraid Ma would overhear. Ma was in her 'Poor-thing-be-kind-that's-what-family-does' mood and Mishti didn't want another lecture. It was all right for her! *She* wasn't being uprooted and thrown out of her most comfortable space.

Riya was much more sympathetic. Like the true friend Mishti knew she was. She cried out and exclaimed and said all the right things.

'Do you know,' she said, 'that's the meanest thing I've ever heard?'

The girls were tucked away behind the school shed. Mishti had been so impatient that she had dragged Riya there at the first gong of the lunch bell. And while Riya ate her sandwiches noisily, Mishti poured out her woes to her friend. How sudden and unfair and disgusting and all the rest till she ran out of adjectives and had to stop to draw breath.

'But Mishti,' Riya began chomping through one of Mishti's chicken rolls, 'why are you so worried? If you don't want her in your house—'

'I don't!'

'Then it's really very easy to get rid of her.' She picked up another chicken roll and bit into it.

'What do you mean?'

'It's easy,' Riya shrugged, spraying some chicken roll on Mishti as she spoke, 'you just have to be terrible to her—really, really obnoxious. Very obnoxious and moan and groan and complain—'

'But, but—how—'

'And *then*,' she eyed the last roll and licked her lips, '*then* they'll send her away—'

Mishti hurriedly bit into the last roll before Riya could grab it. 'But how? And where? Ma said she had nowhere else to go.'

'Oh, there are plenty of places,' said Riya, airily, 'for mad people; or people with handicaps—institutions—you know—'

Mishti shook her head; she didn't.

'Don't worry, Mishti, let her come first. Then we'll work out a plan of action—Munni Hatao, Mishti Bachao!' Riya got up and dusted down her skirt. 'Those rolls were really good.'

Mishti could only look at the crumbs and nod her head.

Chapter 3

Even before Mishti had seen her, she knew Munni had arrived.

There were three suitcases on the landing, the shoe rack had been moved to one side and the sofa was crooked. Piled between the sofa and the dining table were her things: the hundred-piece jigsaw puzzle that she had left half-done on the floor, the cardboard suitcase which she had made and Buboon, sitting on the very top of the pile, grinning crookedly. Everything that had been in Thamma's room, in fact. Shoved, anyhow, out of the way, to make space for Munni! And she had been *that* close to finishing the jigsaw!

'Ma!' she called. 'Ma! I'm home!'

No Ma. Mishti waited, her ears getting hot and the drawing-room clock ticking loudly in her head. Tick-tick-tick-TICK-TICK!

'Ma!' she yelled. 'MA! MA! I'm—'

'Why are you screaming?' Ma poked her head out of Thamma's room. 'Can't you see I'm busy?'

'I'm home!'

'I can see that,' said Ma, crossly. 'Your clothes are on my bed and your food is on the table—eat and then watch TV or something while we finish here.'

'Where's Baba?'

Ma disappeared without another word.

Mishti's clothes were on Ma's bed. *All* of them. Every single piece of clothing that she owned, that had so far been sitting tidily in Thamma's big wooden cupboard.

Eyes smarting, Mishti picked out what she wanted to wear, dropped some on the floor, then walked off without bothering to pick anything up.

Thamma's door was closed. Of course! She would now have to use the other bathroom. The outside bathroom that she always turned up her nose at.

She sniffed hard, her lips trembling. She couldn't—wouldn't—cry. She was almost eleven. If they wanted to throw her out of her room—fine, she wouldn't care either! Not at all! She would show them!

From behind Thamma's door, came a squawk, then a series of grunts, then a thud-thud-thud as if something was being dragged across the floor. Mishti tiptoed closer. What on earth was happening?

But the door, when she gave it a timid push, was locked. And the noise had stopped. Ma and Thamma were talking.

'I'm sorry I had to thrust her on you like this,' Thamma was saying to Ma, 'but really—'

'Aare, don't worry, Ma,' Ma interrupted. 'Why should there be any problem at all? It's fine, no problem—'

'But Joyeeta, the space—'

'Yes, yes, we'll just have to sort that out—'

'And Mishti?'

This time Ma didn't respond quite so readily. Mishti, with her ear pressed to the door, waited eagerly. For Ma to say that yes, it would be very inconvenient for Mishti to live like this and the sooner Munni was moved out, the better—

'Mishti—' Ma started and stopped and started again, 'will just have to lump it. And learn to adjust as we are all going to do. Now let me bring the tea.'

There was a small laugh from Thamma, then the latch clicked as Ma moved to open the door and Mishti fled.

For all of that first day and most of the next, Munni kept to her room. Most of the time, Thamma stayed with her, much to Mishti's chagrin, and Mishti was told to stay away.

'Don't peek just yet,' Baba told her that evening. 'Munni is very unhappy at being in a strange place.

And all of a sudden, she can't really understand what's going on. She's still not really understood about Rani di dying. That's why your thamma is constantly with her. Thamma was the closest to Rani di—the only friend Munni has at the moment.'

Which worked fine for Mishti. Initially, at least. Because all the grown-ups were busy arranging and rearranging things, no one paid any attention to Mishti. Or how long she watched TV. And because no one had had time to cook, they ordered quite a grand meal for dinner.

Which was all good. What was not so good was that she had to sleep with Ma and Baba in their double bed, all squashed up like a sausage. Or that half the night Baba's snores and Ma's constant fidgeting kept her awake.

The next day Riya was all agog to hear the news, but Mishti just shrugged and said she hadn't met Munni yet.

'Maybe today, Thamma said,' she told Riya, 'if she's feeling better. Thamma said she cried all night— almost—and neither of them got any sleep—'

When Mishti finally did meet Munni that evening after school, she was not really sure what to think. Or say. Munni wasn't at all what Mishti had expected. And Mishti wasn't sure *what* she had expected, but certainly it had been nothing like this.

From what Ma had said, Mishti had thought Munni would be like a baby, only much larger. The same size, say as Thamma, whom Baba called a little old woman.

19

But Munni didn't look even remotely baby-like. She looked old, very old, so old that she could easily have been three hundred years old.

She was shrunken and bent and covered in wrinkles. Hundreds and thousands of wrinkles from head to toe. And she was fat and round in the middle with very thin arms and legs, like sticks.

'Come on, Mishti,' said Ma, 'don't gape—'

'Come here, Mishti.' Thamma was next to Munni. 'Come and say hello to Munni.'

There was nothing Mishti wanted less, but she walked over and mumbled, 'Hello.'

'Don't look at the floor please, Mishti.' Ma again.

'Hel-lo!' Mishti looked up and almost shouted.

But there was no answer. Munni's head was bobbing up and down, her straggly hair falling across her eyes and she was muttering to herself. Her fingers were picking at her dress.

'Go and change, Mishti,' Ma said. 'You can make friends with Munni later.'

'Yes,' said Thamma brightly, not looking at Mishti. 'It'll be such fun to have another grandmother, na Mishti rani?'

'Why is she my grandmother?' Mishti asked Baba after dinner.

'Well-ll-ll,' Baba stretched and yawned, 'she is Thamma's sister. Her cousin. My cousin aunt. Your cousin grandmother.'

'I won't have to call her Thamma, will I?'

The grown-ups looked at each other. Ma started to speak, but Thamma rushed in first. 'No, no; much better you call her Munni. She's always been called that—she won't mind.'

That was a relief, thought Mishti that night as she tried to find a comfortable place between Ma and Baba. Easier; like they were the same age. Like someone on the school playground. Equals.

The following day was the start of the Easter break, so Mishti couldn't tell Riya anything about Munni. But that worked well, as it turned out, because by the end of the week she had so much more to tell.

After the first two days, Munni lost all her shyness. Every morning, she would crawl to the green sofa in the drawing room and pull herself up on to it. Specifically on to the single seat that curved around to form a corner at the end. It couldn't have been very easy but she hauled herself up by using the arm of the sofa and squeezed herself on to the seat. It was a tightish fit, because she was plump, but she seemed to prefer it that way, moving her bottom this way and that till she was properly wedged in.

Once settled, she would drink her tea with slurping noises and crunch down her biscuits. Four biscuits, one after the other, the crumbs falling out of her mouth and all down the front of her dress. Sometimes a big piece of biscuit would fall out too and Munni would pick that off her dress and put it back in her mouth, then suck greedily.

'You see, Mishti,' Thamma explained, 'it's because she doesn't have any teeth.'

'None at all?' Mishti wanted to know.

'Well, not many,' Thamma conceded.

Then how did she eat?

Mishti waited for Munni to open her mouth. She saw two or three dirty broken teeth sticking out this way and that. It was difficult to see properly because her face was covered with wrinkles right down to her lips. On top of which her eyes were mismatched, slanting at odd angles, and she had a long nose that twitched when you least expected it.

'Does she talk?' Riya asked breathlessly during break. Mishti had so much to tell her that they had been whispering all morning. All through maths and environmental sciences and value education right up to break time.

'Yes, no—' Mishti stopped. Munni couldn't talk properly, only in half-words and broken sentences.

In the five days that she had been in Mishti's house, she had only said 'Hmm' and 'Mmm mm' and 'Na-na-na'. And 'Hel-lo-lo-lo!' every time she saw Mishti or Ma or Baba. 'She likes to say hello to new people,' Thamma had said.

But strangely, even when she didn't say much, she seemed to understand what was said to her—most times. Other times she shouted and howled and cried so hard that her eyes grew red and her nose watered without stopping.

'But why does she cry?' Riya asked. 'It's not as if you scold her or anything?'

'Thamma said it's because she can't make the words she wants. She says—Thamma says—that Munni is actually very intelligent, but because she can't talk properly—articulate, Thamma said—she gets annoyed and angry. With herself.'

'Does she speak to you much?'

Munni had tried actually, thought Mishti; it was *she* who had ignored her. After that first 'Hello!' episode, Mishti had not really tried at all.

Thamma had introduced them again the next morning. Properly, like grown-ups. 'Look Munni, this is Mishti. Say hello—'

'Hell-loo!' Munni had yipped happily. 'Hell-lo! Hell-lo! Hell-lo-lo-lo!!'

Mishti was sidling off, when Ma caught her. 'Say hello, Mishti.'

'Hello,' snapped Mishti.

'Say "Hello Munni",' Ma insisted. But Mishti wouldn't.

This was most unreal. This shrunken old—*thing!*—on the sofa that looked like an old woman and bawled like a baby. And slobbered all down her mouth, the spittle falling on her lap, on the sofa, on the floor. Mishti was disgusted.

So she just shrugged off Riya's question. 'A little, not really—'

But then the bell rang and they had to run, Riya quickly snatching up the last of Mishti's sandwiches in the rush. There was no more talk of Munni in class, but as they were packing their bags, Riya asked, 'Is the plan still on?'

'Huh? What plan?'

'*You* know,' Riya rolled her eyes, '*the* plan— about *Munni*—'

And because Mishti didn't say anything, she shook her head and said, 'Don't you remember? Munni Hatao, Mishti Bachao!'

'But how—'

'Easy,' Riya fluttered her fingers, 'but I'll have to come and see her first. Like generals, you know, before a battle, they have to know,' her eyes narrowed, 'the lie of the land.'

So, many complex plans were laid in whispers and by dint of some clever timing, Mishti got Ma to agree to Riya's visit.

But Mishti wasn't sure what Riya could actually do. Granted, she was a brilliant plotter, but what could a ten-year-old girl—or two—do against so many grown-ups?

Chapter 4

Riya's visit had been planned for the coming Saturday, so there were still four whole days to go.

Mishti was getting more and more used to sleeping like a sausage at night. She had tried sleeping on one side, throwing a tantrum so that Ma moved to the centre, between Baba and her. And rolled promptly off the bed in the middle of the night, landing on the floor with an undignified thud.

So now she was back in the middle, squashed like a sausage in a hot dog between her parents. How she missed her old bed! Her very own especially-made teak double bed that Thamma had given her. Now it was Munni's. No, she thought angrily, Mishti would never give it to her. She had only *lent* it to Munni, and only for a few days.

But she had been very careful not to say anything about the bed. Or Munni. Riya had warned her how it would be. 'If you keep yelling and screaming and telling everyone how annoyed you are, it won't work.'

'But *you* said I should be obnoxious!'

'Yes, yes, but not *now*! *After* I have seen her and made the plan—only then! Honestly, Mishti, why are you so stupid?'

'Don't call me stupid!' Mishti stamped her foot. 'She lives in *my* house. How will you know more about her just by seeing her for a few minutes?'

'You don't know anything about it,' said Riya with her nose in the air. 'I've already got rid of two ayahs and one tutor! They never dared to come back!'

And with that Mishti had to be content.

Munni, on the other hand, had settled in very well. She drank her tea every morning in the drawing room with the slice of toast that Thamma broke into little pieces. Then she went back to her room for a nap till lunch. Lunch she ate in her room with Thamma in attendance, cutting up her food, feeding her like a baby, then wiping her clean afterwards. Dinner was outside again. On the sofa with a high table that had been bought especially for her. The table came right up to her chin, so she had to eat with her mouth almost disappearing into the bowl. But Ma said that was the most convenient arrangement. A lower table would mean that she would have to bend too much and it would hurt her tummy. Every time she ate, she got food all over her mouth, her chin and sometimes even on her nose, but no one seemed to mind. After she had eaten, she would chortle and gurgle and Thamma would clean her up with a pleased smile and Ma would say, 'Good girl, Munni!', which made her gurgle even harder so that the spit dribbled down even more.

'Like a pig at a trough,' muttered Mishti, viciously. She knew what Ma would say if *she* tried to eat with her chin in a bowl. 'Behave yourself, Mishti! You're grown up now, Mishti!' Only no one cared that Munni—who was grown up, even old—didn't behave like a grown-up.

And to top it all, she crawled. Never before had Mishti seen a crawling grandparent. And one that loved to explore. After those first few days, she crawled everywhere. Regularly and at an astonishing pace. From her bed to the sofa, back to her bed, then to the bathroom. And even to Mishti's secret cave.

A week after Munni's arrival, Mishti had gone back to her favourite pastime of making a cave under the dining table with a mat and some old sarees. The dining table also dated from Thamma's wedding, so like the bed, it was old and high and made of sturdy teak. And very convenient to turn into a cave because it had so much room underneath.

Of course, the cave was only ever a temporary one, but sometimes, Ma let it go on being a cave for a while if she was in a good mood. And Mishti with her favourite book, the cushions off the sofa and her stolen pack of biscuits could read in there for hours.

But today, she had hardly got past the first chapter when there was a *THUD*! outside and some scuffling noises.

The next moment Mishti screamed as Munni poked her head inside.

'Lo-lo-lo-lo!'

'No,' said Mishti at once, 'you can't come in here—go away!'

'Lo-lo-lo-lo!' Munni crawled right inside, right up to her waist.

'No! No!' said Mishti loudly, flapping her hands. 'Go away, go away—shoo-shoo-shoo!'

Munni broke into a wide smile, her eyes disappearing into her cracked face and her broken teeth gaping wide. 'Hell-lo! Hell-lo!'

'Go away!' Mishti sat upright, nearly hitting her head. 'This is *my* cave! Mine!' She pointed at herself. 'Mishti! Mishti! Mishti's cave! Not yours—sHOOO!'

Munni blinked as Mishti's flapping fingers almost caught her nose. Then 'Mit-ti—' she burst out grinning hugely. 'Mit-ti! Hal-lo-lo-lo!'

In the end, it took Thamma and Ma and Baba together to persuade Munni to leave. She seemed to be having such a good time. She crawled out, still booming 'Mit-ti!', her big bottom waddling in time to her cries.

Mishti felt like crying. Her cave had been spoilt, just when she had settled in peacefully. What was that word they had learnt in the English class? Idyll—that's the one; the idyll had been broken. And though Munni had left, her cave was now full of Munni's smell.

Because Munni had a smell. A strong one. Very early on, Mishti had noticed it and remarked on it and been shushed up. But that didn't take the smell away. It was a mixture of sweat and food and other nasty bathroom-type things. A very Munni smell. It went away when Munni had a bath, which was not very often.

Munni hated baths and there were yowls and shrieks and roaring every time Thamma tried to give her one. Then Thamma would come out wet and tired and crying, and Ma would make her a cup of hot tea and pat her on the shoulder and say, 'Never mind, Ma, never mind!'

Ma had taken to Munni like a duck to water. She petted her and patted her on the head and fed her little treats that she would never allow Mishti to have. Extra chocolates, for example, or the last sausage off the plate. Munni loved sausages. Thamma said she'd never eaten them before but they had become her favourite food. Cut up into little pieces, she would pick them off her plate and eat them daintily with her matchstick-like fingers.

'What beautiful fingers she's got!' Ma had once said admiringly. 'Slender, tapering.'

'She puts them up her nose,' Mishti butted in loudly. Which was true; more than once, Mishti had seen Munni with her fingers up her nose, digging. Why did no one else notice? They would notice in a flash if Mishti was the one doing the digging.

And even if her fingers were beautiful, which Mishti very much doubted, her feet were absolutely awful to look at. Withered, twisted and dirty. With thick brown knobs of skin that stood out on her knees and heels and the sides of her ankles. Her toenails were filthy too, filthy and chipped. Yes, all right, she was crawling all the time, but no one told *her* to clean up afterwards.

She was half-scared, half-excited about Riya's visit. The grown-ups didn't know about the 'Munni Hatao, Mishti Bachao' plan, of course, but Riya was very confident of her own powers. Almost as if she could do magic!

Riya arrived dressed as if to go to a party. She was always very well-dressed. Matching frock-hairband-shoes-little handbag. She had even had a mani-pedi for her tenth birthday. Mishti couldn't imagine what Ma would say if *she* asked for one!

And she always had the most bee-yoo-tiful manners. 'Hello aunty, uncle, Thamma!' she would trill as soon as she entered the flat. And then prattle and chat and say 'Thank-yooooo!' at all the right places.

Munni was still in her room when Riya arrived. Shanti didi was cleaning the drawing room so Ma told Mishti to take Riya into their bedroom.

'So difficult in a flat,' murmured Riya in a poor-honey-pretend-grown-up voice. She lived in a laa-aa-aarge house, of course. 'Where shall I sit?'

'Oh anywhere,' Mishti gestured vaguely, 'the chair or the bed—or the—'

'The bed? Should I? I mean, these are outside clothes. Mummy is *vaairy* strict about sitting on the bed with outside clothes—*not* sitting, I mean—'

'Mishti!' Ma called and Mishti rushed out thankfully. Riya was still talking to herself.

Mishti had badgered Ma into baking her special cupcakes for the occasion. Big fat ones with coloured icing and sprinkles on top. Mishti had asked Ma to make an extra batch because 'Riya loves them'.

'She's just greedy, Mishti,' Ma had replied.

'But Ma!'

'Any child who eats eight cupcakes in one go— eight!—can only be called greedy! Don't you think I know that she eats all your tiffin?'

But she had baked the cupcakes anyway, and now they sat proudly on the table, tempting and fresh.

'Two-three-five-six-seven—Ma?'

'Yes?'

'Can't we have some more?'

'There aren't any more.'

'But I told you to bake an extra batch!'

'And I didn't. Have you seen the size of these things? You have seven between the two of you—that's three-and-a-half each—' Ma was very good at maths inside her head.

'But she'll eat them all!' Mishti wailed.

'Yes, well.' Ma shrugged in a that's-your-problem way. 'She's your guest.'

'Give me one more, Ma, just one!'

'No, there aren't any extra ones.'

'But-but—' Mishti could do maths too. 'Seven for us—and you, Baba, Thamma and Munni—that's eleven. That's one extra . . .' Mishti helped Ma with her baking so she knew that there were always twelve cupcakes in a batch.

'No, it isn't,' Ma snapped. 'Munni gets two—now, will you go before I lose my temper?'

Mishti went. There would be no arguing, she knew. Not with Ma in that mood. But she was furious. Munni would get two! Two cupcakes! More than anyone else!

She poured her heart out to Riya, with all the sums and the calculations and the unfairness of it all. Riya heard it all through with sympathetic chomping noises, then said, 'Never mind, you can always throw a tantrum for some more—these are truly scrumptious!'

She stretched out her hand for the very last cupcake on the plate. Just in time, Mishti noticed and made a grab for it as well. After a brief struggle, she came away with some crumbs.

'Yumm.' Riya stood and shook the crumbs off her lap on to the rug. 'Even better than the shop ones. Now, I'm ready! Shall we go and see her?'

35

Mishti nodded. Sulkily, because she had managed only a few cupcake crumbs, not even a whole one. But there was no time to complain. She heard the thuds and the grunts which signalled Munni's arrival into the drawing room and really the MHMB plan needed to be put into action without any more delay.

'Come on,' she urged. 'Munni's already come and—' It struck her that she hadn't described Munni properly to Riya. 'You don't know what she looks like. I was quite frightened the first time I saw her . . .'

'Oh, *I'm* never frightened of anybody. The two tutors and the ayah were quite ugly and horrible, but I wasn't scared at all. It feels quite exciting, actually.' She gave a delighted wriggle. 'Come on, come on, I can't wait!' she said as she hurried out. 'It'll be very easy. Just you wait and see. Do you know, with the first tutor, I—'

But what she had done with the first tutor, Mishti would never know. Because Riya stopped suddenly and Mishti bumped into her and nearly fell.

'Oh, there you are,' said Ma. 'Come and say hello. Riya, this is Munni; Munni, this is Riya, Mishti's special friend. Say hello.'

But Riya couldn't say a word. Her eyes were popping right out of her head. She stood where she was, goggling at her first sight of Munni.

Munni was sitting in her favourite place on the sofa, fitted round and tight as always. She was eating cupcakes. A big chocolate one was in her left hand and with the right she was cramming the purple one into her mouth. Crumbs were raining down on to her lap, the sofa, the table—everything. But no one noticed. Once she'd got the purple one inside—or what little she could—she started to rock happily, slobbering all over her chin as she tried to chew.

'Say hello, Riya,' Ma said again, but Riya had frozen.

Ma frowned. 'Say hello, Munni,' she said instead. 'Look, that's Riya,' she pointed. 'Wave at Riya?' She gave a little wave.

'HALL-LLOOO!' shrieked Munni at once. 'Hal-lo-hal-lo-lo-lo!' She raised a hand and cracked her mouth open in a wide grin. 'HELL-LO-LO!' she yelled again, so strongly that the half-chewn mass of sodden cupcake flew right out and across the room towards Riya.

Riya came to life and screamed. Screeched and howled and wailed much louder than Munni had ever done.

'Oooooh! Monster! Monster! Monster! Oooooh! Oooooh! Oooooh!' She rushed back into the bedroom, followed by Mishti. Then she fell on to the bed in a hysterical fit and shuddered and shook and trembled for a good fifteen minutes. By the end of which time, Mishti had gone to Ma for help, afraid that her friend had fallen ill.

'What a silly child!' said Ma, crossly. 'Making a fuss like that over nothing.'

'It's not nothing—' Mishti started to say, but Ma had disappeared into the bedroom.

'It's all *your* fault,' she whispered fiercely to Munni, who had now started on the chocolate cupcake.

Munni peered at Mishti with her twinkling slits of eyes. 'Mit-ti-ti-ti-ti-ti!' she said in a pleased voice. 'Mit-ti-ti!'

'Oh *you!*' Mishti flounced away to see what was happening.

Riya was in the chair, she noticed at once, not stretched across the bed as if she was about to die. And she had stopped crying though there was snot all over her cheeks and down the front of her pretty dress. Ma was holding her by one shoulder and trying to wipe her face at the same time. Which was not very easy because even though she had stopped crying, she kept moaning and wheezing and whining all through the wiping.

Finally, even Ma had enough. 'Stop it, Riya!' She gave her a little shake. 'There's nothing to cry about.'

At once, Riya began to howl again. 'Oh-oh-oh! Monster-monster-ooo-ooo-ooooh!'

And that was all the sense that could be got out of her for the rest of the visit.

Chapter 5

Riya's visit was not a success.

Even Mishti had to concede that it had done nothing to further any grand plans. Secretly, she was quite disappointed with Riya, but of course, she couldn't say so.

Ma was openly annoyed. 'I've always thought her very silly. Pretending and posing and copying her elders and giving herself airs. No one is deceived, Mishti. She may be your best friend, but she's also very annoying. She should be thoroughly ashamed of herself, throwing a fit like that—'

But Riya, when Mishti met her on Monday, was far from feeling ashamed. Instead, she looked very pleased with herself, dancing up to Mishti first thing in the morning and chirping, 'Well, did it work?'

'What?' asked Mishti, surprised.

'The plan, the plan!'

'What plan?'

'Uff, Mishti, why are you so stupid? Can't you see I did it all for you? To show them how scary and monstrous Munni is?'

'So your screaming—all that drama—'

'Was just an act! You didn't *really* think I was scared, did you?' And she skipped away to class.

Mishti didn't quarrel with Riya because she wanted Riya to stay her best friend. But after that day, she didn't ask her for any advice. The MHMB plan died a natural death.

And it *was* getting easier at home. Things had fallen into a routine, as things do even after the biggest earth-shaking changes. Everyone had found ways and means to adjust to Munni in their home and their lives.

Even Mishti.

Oh, she was still annoyed by the whole Munni situation. At the fact that she had to move in with her parents and that Thamma spent a lot of time with Munni these days. But she wasn't disgusted by Munni any more—by the crumbs on the sofa, or the spittle running down her chin or the occasional finger up her nose. Sometimes, she even had to remind herself to remain annoyed with Munni. 'It's war!' she would tell herself, 'war, war!' and then meekly carry over Munni's cup of tea when Ma handed it to her.

Munni, of course, had no problems at all—she loved living with the family. Thamma was very pleased. 'I didn't expect her to adjust so quickly. I'm so relieved—

my Mishti rani has been such a good girl.' She pulled Mishti close. 'Generous and kind and welcoming.'

Mishti said nothing, thinking about the failed MHMB conspiracy. She picked up a biscuit and held it out to Munni.

'Toh-toh-to-do-do!' said Munni, stuffing the biscuit into her mouth and holding up two crooked fingers.

That was the thing with Munni, she always wanted two of everything. *Asked* for two of everything anyway. Biscuits, sweets, chocolates, even the special cheese puffs that Ma brought home one day. The cheese puffs were gigantic. No one could possibly have managed more than one, but Ma only said, 'Have one, Munni, and then I'll give you the other one—'

But there were only five in the box—one each. Mishti hurriedly bit into hers. Whose cheese puff would Ma give Munni?

But Munni, it turned out, was very sensible. When she had finally polished off her cheese puff, Ma asked her, 'Do you want another one?'

'N-no-no-no-no,' she replied at once. 'Yummm', which was her way of saying she was full.

So everyone had a whole cheese puff and the grown-ups chuckled over their tea.

'She's not greedy,' Ma said, 'it's only her way—'

But not everyone understood that. Not even if they were relatives, and grown-ups in the bargain.

Tinu mashi had come to visit them on one of her flying trips from Bangalore. She had brought sweets for Thamma—Mysore pak, which was her favourite—and some special chocolates.

'Ta-da!' She fished them out of her bag with a flourish. 'One for you and one for Munni.'

'Toh-toh-to-do-do,' said Munni, immediately, grinning with her dirty broken teeth.

'Yes, yes, for both of you. One for Mishti and one for you—'

'TOH!' roared Munni, holding up two fingers like a flag. 'Toh-toh-TOH!'

'She means two,' said Mishti helpfully. 'Two chocolates.'

'Toh-toh-to-do-do-DO!' Munni nodded vigorously.

'Oh, but—' Tinu mashi fluttered her hands helplessly. 'I got only two. I don't have any more.'

'Never mind, Tinu,' Thamma started to say. 'Next time—'

But Tinu mashi went right on. 'And anyway, Munni, you mustn't be greedy—those are big chocolates and very rich. If you're greedy, you'll be sick. Bad girl, Munni!'

'She's not greedy,' Mishti interrupted without a thought, 'it's only her way—'

Later that night, Mishti thought, how strange it was that no one had ticked her off. After Ma's many strictures on not interrupting and being polite to guests and all the rest of it. Tinu mashi had hiccupped and stopped, Ma and Thamma had grinned secretly at each other and Munni had started again, 'Toh-toh-toh-toh-doh!'

That did *not* mean that she had become friends with Munni. In spite of the failure of the MHMB plan, she would *not* get used to Munni. They lived in the same house, that was all. Just like the broken toaster or the rubber plant or the two lizards that lived in the kitchen.

And sometimes, Mishti had to admit, Munni even had her uses. Like the time when Ma was lecturing Mishti for not completing her geography homework and Munni started bawling so loudly that everyone rushed to see what had happened. Geography was conveniently forgotten.

She was good as a scavenger too. A finder of lost things. There was the precious golden marker which Mishti had lost almost immediately after Ma had bought it and thought she had left it at school. She hadn't told Ma, of course, only nodded when Ma had asked her whether it was working all right. A whole week later, Munni came crawling into her cave rolling the marker in front of her. She came right in, rolled the marker towards Mishti and grinned.

'Where did you find it?' asked Mishti, even before she said thank you. But Munni didn't say. She only cackled 'Mit-ti!' and backed out at top speed.

Mishti didn't mind Munni in her cave any more. For one, she didn't stay too long. On some days, she would just poke her head through the curtains at the entrance. And stay there, looking like a stuffed tiger's head in a hunting lodge. On other days, she did not even enter the cave, though Mishti could hear her go thup-thup-thup, all over the flat.

There were still times when Munni cried. Even after many months with Mishti and her family. Bawled her head off with her mouth wide open and her tongue hanging out and the little fleshy bit on the roof of her mouth swinging like a mad pendulum. With so many tears that her frock got all wet and her withered face screwed up tight so that her eyes disappeared into its cracks. Then Ma or Thamma would wipe her face with a wet cloth and pet and cajole or even scold till she shut up.

'She misses Rani di,' sighed Thamma the first time it happened, 'and she can't really understand why she's had to leave her home and come to live with strangers. Or where Rani di's gone. Usually, she's good, but sometimes—perhaps when she's thinking too hard—it just gets too much for her. Poor thing!'

It wasn't as if Munni was mad, as Ma repeatedly pointed out, or an idiot. She would say 'Hmm' or 'Na-na' at the most appropriate moments. Once she even said, 'Velll-baaad!' when she didn't like some chicken Thamma had cooked and refused to touch what was left on her plate.

It still didn't mean that Mishti was willing to be friends. She was just tolerating Munni in her home, though she dared not say it aloud except in the bathroom. Ma had looked like a thunderstorm when Mishti had said something similar in the beginning. 'This is her home now, Mishti, get that clear. And she is as much your grandmother as Thamma. Do you hear me?'

Mishti heard all right, but didn't pay attention. At school, Riya told gruesome tales about Munni Monster, the fearsome creature who had come to live in Mishti's house. But Mishti soon learned to laugh them off by pretending she didn't care at all and really, Riya was a silly coward for being so scared. Needless to say, Riya was no longer welcome to Mishti's house any more. Or to her tiffin.

Then, one day, Thamma caught a cold. It was a severe cold with a runny nose and a continuous hacking cough that troubled Mishti no end. Thamma's eyes were red, her nose was rubbed raw from too much blowing and she looked awful.

Ma and Baba kept asking Thamma how she was feeling and dosing her with all sorts of medicines till, at last, she became very cross and refused to take any more. 'Don't fuss like that,' she said, 'it's only a tiny cold and it'll disappear before you know it. And it's only because—' She stopped, looking guilty.

'Because?' prompted Baba.

'Because-because,' Thamma rolled her eyes. 'Because —oh, I had a shower late in the night on Sunday . . .'

She said it very lamely, as if she was making it up on the spur of the moment. Mishti knew that guilty tone well enough—she used it herself all the time.

Ma looked at Thamma thoughtfully, but didn't say anything. That night, Mishti heard her slipping out of their room. To check on Thamma, she thought, snuggling deeper into the blanket. The next morning she understood why.

'You're sleeping on the floor,' said Ma to Thamma. 'In winter, too. That's why your cold won't go. All that talk of a late shower was—'

'Bunkum,' put in Mishti. It was her most recent favourite word—she loved the sound of it.

'An excuse.' Ma ignored the interruption. 'But why? Why are you sleeping on the floor when that huge bed is lying empty—half of it anyway?'

Thamma clucked and put down her mug of tea.

'Munni isn't used to sharing a bed. Even in her own home, she had a single bed all to herself. She shared a room with Rani di, but she had her own bed.'

'Why didn't you tell us?' Baba wanted to know.

'I thought it would sort itself out as she settled down. The first few nights were the most difficult. I thought she was crying and shouting for Rani di, but then, I realized it wasn't that. She screamed every time I tried to get on to the bed. But it's fine now—she goes to sleep without any trouble.'

'But you're the one who's falling ill,' Ma pointed out.

'It's nothing.' Thamma pushed her plate away and got up. 'I'll be fine.'

Ma and Baba looked at each other, but didn't say anything just then. Mishti heard them whispering late at night, but too softly for her to hear.

Three days later, Mishti came home from school to find an army of men in the flat. Ma bundled her off into the bedroom. There were thuds and banging and grunts and huffing and loud voices and the screech of the dining table pushed back and forth.

A good one hour of banging went by before Ma opened the door and said, 'Okay, Mishti, you can come out now—'

'Come and see, Mishti.' Thamma was beaming. 'I want you to be the first one to see.' She sounded so excited that Mishti hurried straight over.

'See.' She pointed inside her bedroom. 'Doesn't it look nice?'

Mishti peeped in. There were two sleek single beds, spanking new, one on each side of the door, pushed back against the wall.

'Aren't they smart, Mishti?' Thamma was babbling in her excitement. 'Look how little space they take up. And look,' she bent down, 'there's this huge drawer for storage.'

'Where's the bed?' blurted out Mishti.

'The bed?'

'The old one, Thamma, the big one—my one, the one I dusted every day! *My* bed!'

'Oh that—' Thamma looked helplessly around. 'That . . .'

'We had to give it away, Mishti.' Ma came in. Mishti was sure she had been listening outside the door. 'Thamma couldn't carry on sleeping on the floor, could she?'

'But she could sleep on *that* bed, Ma—'

'You know why she couldn't, Munni wouldn't let her—'

'Then Munni could have slept in a single bed on her own and Thamma could have slept on the big bed. Why did you have to give it away?'

'Mishti—' Ma closed her eyes in her 'Mishti-you're-annoying-me' look. Then she turned her gently by the shoulders and swept her hand around the room. 'Where is the space, Mishti? Is this room really big enough? The old bed itself was a tightish fit—a single bed on top of that would just not—'

'But it was *my* bed!' Mishti began to cry. 'My very own bed that Thamma gave me. Why couldn't it have come into our room?'

'Because we already have a bed there, Mishti,' Ma dragged her outside, 'and that room is even smaller than this one—'

'Mit-ti-ti!'

Munni was in her usual corner on the sofa, rocking with glee. 'Mit-ti-ti! Mit-tiiiii!'

'I hate you!' Mishti stamped her foot, forgetting her tears in her rage. 'I hate you—you—monster! I wish you were dead! You hear me? Dead! Dead! *Dead!*'

Chapter 6

After that, it was war.

WAR.

In capital letters. Even though Mishti was pulled up for bad behaviour. Even though Thamma cuddled her and cuddled her, again and again, and tried to make things better with all sorts of promises. Mishti would not be cuddled. And she would not be consoled.

In her grief, she even made friends with Riya again. 'None of this would have happened if Thamma hadn't got herself a cold.'

'Yeff.' Riya nodded, chewing noisily. 'Very inconsiredate.'

'What?'

'It means,' Riya emptied her mouth in one big gulp, 'that she didn't think about you.'

'No one thinks about me,' said Mishti, gloomily.

'Don't worry.' Riya swooped down on the last mini quiche Lorraine. 'I've got a plan—MHMB Part 2! If they won't think about you, you'll have to force them to!'

A long discussion followed. And after dinner, Mishti put the plan into action.

Just as she was leaving the table, she announced, looking straight at Thamma, 'I want a bed—'

The grown-ups swivelled around to look at her.

'A single bed,' she said again, loudly. 'Like a bunk bed—I can't sleep squashed in like a sausage any more.'

'Oh, poor Mishti,' Thamma began, but Baba stopped her.

'One minute, Ma. What is the matter, Mishti?' he asked. 'Why this sudden longing for a bed?'

Mishti looked around the table, thinking of Riya's words. Ma was beginning to look furious, so she fixed her eyes on Thamma, took a deep breath and launched into the pre-planned speech.

'I am too old now to sleep squashed between my parents. I have grown up and I need my own space like everyone else and it is inconsiredate—'

Baba spluttered and quickly started coughing.

Mishti glared at him.

'It is inconsiredate and—and—' She struggled to remember the words that Riya had drummed into her. But nothing would come. Ma was giggling and Baba was screwing up his mouth and even Thamma was chuckling openly.

'It's not fair!' she cried at last, very loudly so that they would know she meant it. 'I *want* a bed of my own. It's horrible having to share with Ma and Baba in their tiny bedroom and use the outside bathroom in the cold and—and—*why* can't I have my own bed?' She ended on a wail.

Ma got up and came to put her arm around Mishti. She wasn't angry any more or laughing, just a little sad. But Mishti shrugged off Ma's arm. She didn't want to be comforted like a child, she just wanted her own way. Which meant her own bed. The soonest it could be arranged.

'Poor Mishti, I'm so sorry about all this.' Thamma reached out to Mishti.

'Thamma, no!' Mishti flung her arm back and nearly stamped her foot again. 'Stop treating me like a baby—I'm nearly eleven years old! I'm not a baby to be petted and consoled with empty promises!'

That last grand-sounding bit was Riya's. Mishti had remembered it just in time.

'Sit down,' Baba said so suddenly, it made her jump.

'Sit down,' he said again when she didn't move. Firmly. Calmly but firmly.

'If I understand you,' he said as soon as Mishti had sat down, 'you object to being treated like a child. In which case, you feel, perhaps, that you ought to be treated like an adult?'

Her eyes on Baba, Mishti nodded.

'Right—' Baba pushed his plate away. 'Here is the grown-up version of the answer to your question—You can't have a new bed.' He looked Mishti square in the face. 'You can't have a new bed because we can't afford it. We've just bought two new beds. There is no money to buy yet another one. We are all sorry that Thamma's bed had to be given away, but—before you ask—we couldn't have accommodated it anywhere else in this flat. We don't live in a palace—'

'Aah, Rajat—' Thamma stopped Baba. 'Why are you bothering the child with all this?'

'Because she doesn't want to be a child any more, Ma, she wants to grow up.' Baba was glaring at Thamma now. 'If she's a grown-up, she'll have to know these things. Think about money worries the way we do!'

He left the table, scraping the chair back noisily.

Mishti got up too, feeling a little wobbly. Her eyes were hot, and she sniffed hard a few times so that the tears wouldn't flow out through her nose.

I am too old to cry, she told herself fiercely. And anyway, why should I cry! It's their fault—I am right and they are wrong!

She kept quiet on the subject after that, because she knew from experience that nothing would change. And if she didn't cry, perhaps the grown-ups would be pleased that she wasn't making a fuss and think that she didn't mind any more.

How wrong they would be, thought Mishti, as she watched Ma and Thamma chatting and laughing over tea and Munni spilling crumbs down her frock. They hadn't a clue. That bed had meant the world to her. Never ever in her life had she been given a thing like that for her very own—a precious grown-up thing. And she had kept her promise—she had, she had! Never ever before this had she dusted anything in her life. Till Thamma had given her the bed and made her promise. She—Mishti—had kept her promise, but the grown-ups hadn't. They never did. They gave you things, then took them away.

'Or they promise,' said Riya, the next day, 'and then forget about it—like totally forget, I mean. I was supposed to get an MP3 player—with headphones—if I didn't fail in maths. And what happened?'

'What?' asked Mishti with interest, giving her the last cream roll.

'They ignored me, that's what happened. Although I got fifty-six this time instead of thirty-six like last term—see! That's enough for maths, isn't it?'

Mishti, who had scored ninety-two, nodded. 'But why didn't they give you the player?'

'Because,' Riya licked some cream off her thumb, 'they forgot! They patted my head and said "Thank god!" and "Finally!" and "Well done!" and forgot!'

'But didn't you ask them for it?'

'Of course I did! They said yes, yes, sure, sure and forgot again! Empty promises! All inconsiredate and empty promises!'

'So now?'

'So now nothing! I don't bother any more with marks or rubbish—what's the use?'

She went back to licking her fingers.

'So what should I do now?' asked Mishti, putting her tiffin box away.

'Just continue with the plan, what else? MHMB 2!'

Which really only involved annoying her parents and asking them for all the things that Munni wanted. And pointing out all the odd things that Munni did. This last one was guaranteed to click, Riya told her.

'Because they're all sorry for Munni,' she said seriously, 'they don't really see how disgusting she is. But if you can show them, *then* they'll understand. *Then* they'll see how they really can't keep her in the house any more—'

Mishti came home from school with plenty to think about. For the next few days, she was quiet, absent-minded, even forgetful. Ma asked her a few times if she was unwell, but Mishti shook her head. She wasn't sick, just thinking.

After five days of thinking hard, she finally decided that Riya was right. Munni was disgusting and horrible and her parents had to be shown that, if they couldn't see it for themselves.

So the next time Ma gave her biscuits with her evening milk, Mishti ate them noisily and clumsily in classic Munni-style, breaking them into bits and dropping crumbs all down her T-shirt.

Ma didn't notice at first; she was chatting with Thamma. Mishti crunched louder and louder and slurped her milk and clattered the glass on the table till Ma looked up with a frown.

'Mishti,' she said sharply, 'why are you making such a racket?'

Mishti paid no attention, although she was feeling a little scared. But Riya had told her very strictly to follow this part of the plan. The plan would never work if she didn't make a big enough mess—a *disgusting* enough mess.

'Mishti! What on earth are you doing?' Ma had come over to look.

Mishti finished her milk, carefully upending the glass so that the last drops fell down her neck, then rolled the glass away from her and wiped her mouth with the back of her hand.

'Mishti!' She flinched at the horror in Ma's voice. 'Have you gone mad?'

Mishti brushed down her T-shirt as she got up from the table, making sure all the crumbs fell on the floor and looked at Ma.

'I'm waiting for an answer.'

'Nothing, Ma.' Mishti shrugged, although her heart was beginning to thud. 'I'm just finishing up my milk and biscuits . . .'

'Like this?' A finger pointed to the mess.

This was the moment. Mishti straightened up.

'You don't mind when Munni does it.' She put her chin up and waited for Ma to explode.

But the explosion never came. Ma just stood there looking at Mishti keenly as if seeing her for the first time. She didn't say anything, just stood still in the silence, with the clock going tick-tick-tick in the background.

'Never mind, never mind.' Thamma came bustling up. 'I'll clean it all up. Ore baba, Mishti—go and change at once! You'll catch a chill with your clothes all wet like that—'

Still Ma didn't say anything. She put out a hand to stop Thamma, then turned to Mishti. 'Clean it up,' she said very quietly. Then she went back to the sofa, taking Thamma with her.

Mishti whooshed in relief. It had gone rather well, she thought, as a first step, except now she had to clear up the mess she had made. Which was all right really. She was used to it. Right from the time she had been little, Ma had been very strict about cleaning up after herself. Which meant, of course, that she learnt very quickly not to make any more of a mess than was necessary.

But she didn't say that to Riya when she reported the success of the plan. Riya had very different ideas about making messes and clearing them up—Mishti didn't want to be laughed at.

Over aloo parathas the next day, they plotted. Long and complicated plans in great detail. Mishti was so pleased at how well the plan had worked that she let Riya have three of the four aloo parathas. Midway through the last one, Riya belched and put the half-chewed bit back in Mishti's tiffin box, but today, Mishti didn't mind even that.

Once Mishti had understood what she needed to do, it was simple. Simply a question of carrying out a succession of well-laid plans. One day, it was pulling her hair repeatedly like Munni did. Or rock to and fro on a dining table chair screaming 'Lol-lol-lol!' right in the middle of Thamma's favourite TV programme. Or deliberately digging her nose while eating her dinner. Not with the same hand, as Munni did, because this last one even she found disgusting enough.

The adults watched but didn't really say much after that very first time, which puzzled Mishti. It wasn't as if they didn't notice, Mishti could tell. It was as if they were ignoring her on purpose. Like a bug, thought Mishti resentfully, rocking hard all the while. 'Lol-lol-lol!'

So she redoubled her efforts as Riya said she must do while discussing newer plans behind the school shed.

'Try harder, Mishti,' she urged, 'they must be *made* to take notice!'

Mishti thought hard and concentrated and thought and thought and came up with a little plan of her own.

Munni loved socks. She had a whole collection of extremely dirty mismatched socks that she kept stuffed inside her bottom drawer and never let out of her sight. They were horribly smelly because they had never been washed, but that wasn't for want of trying. Munni simply refused to let them out of her sight. She screamed whenever anyone tried to pick them up, even Thamma. Every morning, she would fish out two—any two, usually odd—then put them on with great gusto whilst sitting on the sofa.

'They don't match,' Mishti had said the first time, pointing to Munni's feet. One sock was bright red, the other a deep magenta with black stripes. Munni had only grinned and wiggled her toes and yelled, 'Mit-ti-ti-ti!'

Mishti had only two pairs of coloured socks, all the others were white for school. So feeling very very daring and also a little scared, she opened Baba's sock drawer. Not that Baba had very many pairs either, but at least, they were all coloured. She sneaked out two at random, then slammed the drawer shut, her heart thumping louder than the slammed drawer.

That evening, she finally had her wish. Baba was in a good mood because he had come home unexpectedly early. He was relaxed and laughing and in the middle

of telling a funny story when he suddenly caught sight of Mishti's feet.

For a whole minute there was silence; as if the mute button on the TV remote had been suddenly pressed hard. Thamma and Ma looked at Baba in bewilderment, even Munni stopped rocking.

'Why are you wearing socks, Mishti?' Baba asked finally. 'My socks?'

Mishti held her feet up. 'Don't they look nice, Baba? See!'

'It's April, Mishti—nearly May. Why are you wearing socks at home? My office socks?'

'They're much nicer than mine. I only have white ones for school and my outside ones are so boooooring.' She drew out the word in the whiny babyish tone Riya used all the time.

Baba had stopped looking comfortable and relaxed.

'It still doesn't explain why you've taken my socks without permission! Two odd socks at that which means two pairs are now useless till you deign to give them up.'

Ma put a hand on Baba's arm. 'Mishti—'

Mishti shrugged and dragged them off her feet. 'You don't say anything when Munni wears them—'

At the sound of her name, Munni screeched in delight, her toothless grin plastered all over her face. 'Mit-ti-ti-ti! Mit-ti-ti-ti! Mit-ti-ti-ti!'

Before anyone could say another word, Ma took Mishti by the shoulder and propelled her out of the room.

'Why are you doing this, Mishti?' she asked as soon as they were in the bedroom. 'Why this constant competition with Munni?'

Her voice was so kind that Mishti wanted to hug her fiercely and spill out all the truth. How neglected she had been feeling ever since Munni came to stay. MHMB 1 and then MHMB 2, because she was so devastated about the bed—her bed! And how she just wanted to cry with her head in Ma's lap and make everything go back to how it was before Munni came. Just Ma, Baba, Thamma and her. And her bed.

'Tell me, Mishti.' Ma pulled her gently down. 'What's troubling you?'

Mishti looked at the floor. She wanted the lump in her throat to go away, but it just grew bigger. Desperate to cry, she began to bite her lip; desperate to just cry like a baby and blabber out everything to Ma like she used to. And snuggle into Ma's side and let Ma cuddle her and smooth away all her problems.

Ma was stroking Mishti's hair, something she had not done in a long, long time. 'My Mishti is not like this new naughty Mishti. My Mishti is a good child, a happy child, not unhappy and bitter and troubled inside herself.'

How did Ma know she had been unhappy? That, had Munni not come, there would have been no need for this terrible naughty behaviour? Did that mean that

Riya was wrong and her parents actually understood her plight?

'Don't give in,' she suddenly heard Riya's warning inside her head. 'If you give up or tell them the truth or cry or anything, the plan will totally fail! Grown-ups can talk you out of anything!'

She pulled away from Ma's side, swallowing her tears and the lump in her throat. But Ma didn't let her go.

'Say something, Mishti; we know it's been difficult for you lately. It's been difficult for all of us. But we hate to see you behaving like this—it upsets us and you know it makes you unhappy.'

Finally, Mishti had to burst. 'I won't be happy!' she blurted out. 'I can't be happy!'

'But why? What is so wrong?'

'Munni! Munni is what's wrong!' She pushed herself away from Ma. Would they never understand? 'She's taken over my room, my house, my bed, my—my—my—my everything!'

Ma sighed. A tired little sigh. 'Would you believe it's been difficult for all of us? Living with Munni—with someone who has special needs—is not at all the same thing as just visiting them once in a while. We've all had to adjust, trust me—even Thamma.'

'Then make her go away, Ma,' Mishti said eagerly. 'Make her go away to some place—some institu—something. And then it'll be all right again. Like before.'

Ma shook her head. 'That would be cruel, Mishti—you don't really mean that. Those places are for people who have no one to look after them—no family, no friends. Would you really be happy knowing your grandmother is in a place like that?'

But Mishti just wouldn't listen. 'I don't care, Ma! Send her away! Please, please, please send her away!'

'I'm sorry, Mishti,' Ma stood up and there were tears in her eyes too, 'but we can't do that.'

'Then I won't be good!' Mishti screamed. 'I won't be good or kind or nice or anything! I won't listen! To you or Thamma or anybody! I hate her! Munni Monster! I wish she had never come! I wish she was dead, dead, *dead*!'

Chapter 7

A month later, Munni fell ill.

It was the height of summer and plants and people were all wilting in the heat. There was only one air conditioner in Mishti's flat and that was in Thamma's room. Thamma and Mishti used it sparingly—usually only at night—and when the heat was completely unbearable, Ma and Baba came in and slept on the floor of Thamma's room. It had been bought two years ago and the plan had been to save up and buy another one soon for Ma's bedroom. Now, of course, there was no question of buying another air conditioner or of anyone else sleeping in Thamma's room. Munni's screeches would have kept all the neighbours awake.

Munni's illness started with the sniffles. At the time, Thamma wasn't too worried.

'It's only because the AC is right on top of her head,' she said, 'and she throws off her cover—it'll go away, don't worry.'

Four days later, the sniffle became a head cold and then turned into a raging fever.

Munni was miserable. She moaned and cried and thrashed about in her bed. All day Mishti heard her go khurr-khurr-khurr in a harsh cough that could be heard all over the flat. She refused to leave her room, refused to crawl around, refused to eat, refused to do anything but cry 'Di-di-di-di-di-'.

Thamma was with her almost constantly, trying to feed her and make her comfortable. She came out only to have her own meals and sometimes not even that. Ma and Baba looked at each other with grim faces and talked constantly in whispers. Even Mishti didn't really want to put any new MHMB plans into action. She played or read quietly by herself and ate without any fuss. But everyone was too worried to notice even that.

Then, on the sixth day, just as they thought she was getting better, Munni started wheezing again. This time she couldn't even lie flat because the cough kept getting caught in her throat and she rocked and gasped desperately trying to get her breath.

Day and night, Ma and Thamma were so busy with her that they didn't have time for anything else. Hot sponges, cold sponges, steam breathing, eucalyptus oil; nothing seemed to work. Baba offered to take leave, but they shook their heads at him and said, 'Not now—maybe later.' Even Mishti had to stay home one day because there was no one to take her to school.

Baba had left at his usual time, much much before Mishti woke up.

'Why aren't you taking her to the hospital, Ma?' Mishti asked in a quiet moment after lunch. Munni had just vomited all over herself and Thamma had sent Ma out to eat lunch while she cleaned her up. They had started taking turns to do things for Munni, because as Thamma said, it was too much for one person alone. And if Ma or Thamma also fell ill, they would be in real trouble.

Ma rubbed her hands over her face and Mishti thought how grey and tired she looked. All because of Munni, she thought again. There had been nothing but trouble since Munni came.

'We may have to in the end.' Ma leaned forward and put her face in her hands. 'Let's see.'

'But you're all getting so tired and upset, Ma. Put her in a hospital and the doctors and nurses can look after her there—'

'Let's see.' Ma stood up. 'Now I must go back so that Thamma can have her lunch.'

That very night Munni stopped breathing. Only for a few seconds, Ma told her later, but she became so blue and lifeless that Thamma screamed in panic and Ma and Baba rushed to her room. They had to shake her and slap her and throw water on her face many times before she snorted and choked and came back to life. That decided Baba.

'I'm not waiting any longer, Ma,' he told Thamma who was crying. 'She'll die if we don't do something.'

Mishti remembered the rest of the night in a sleepy confused half-on half-off haze. The ambulance men kept them waiting nearly an hour before they arrived with their blaring sirens and flashing lights. Baba was pacing up and down in front of the sofa, shouting down the phone every five minutes. Ma and Thamma were with Munni, holding her up and making sure she didn't stop breathing again.

Mishti had been told to stay in the bedroom. There was no time for talk. Ma gave her a quick hug when she came in to change. 'Be a good girl, we'll be back soon.'

After Ma and Baba had left in the ambulance, Thamma came in. She had stopped crying but Mishti had never seen her so upset before. She didn't say much, just put her arm around Mishti and stayed like that. There were so many questions Mishti wanted to ask, but she understood she would have to wait till Ma came back.

The whole house was very grim the next morning. The sun was shining fiercely outside, but it was as if a grey winter cloud had come in and draped itself over everything. Nobody talked much. It was Saturday so Mishti didn't have to go to school. Baba had taken a day off too—he and Ma had returned from the hospital only at breakfast time. It should have felt like a holiday with all of them at home, but it didn't.

Ma was sitting back with her eyes closed, while Baba told Thamma what the doctors had said. Munni had to be put on a breathing machine in a special ward for very sick people.

'The critical care doctor was very angry,' he told Thamma. 'He said if we had admitted her earlier, she would not have needed the ventilator.' His face looked like Mishti's after a bout of crying.

Thamma patted Baba on the head. 'You've done all you could.'

'No, Ma,' Baba sighed, 'maybe not. Maybe we could have—'

'There's no point thinking about that now,' Ma cut in, her eyes still closed. 'We must concentrate on how to get her better—nothing else—it's one of the best hospitals in the city.'

Baba sighed again. 'You know she has no insurance?'

'Yes, Rani di had told me. More than once,' Thamma replied. 'How she had tried and tried and tried. Year after year, she had gone to every insurance company she could think of—private and otherwise. But no one accepted Munni.'

'It's disgusting.' Ma's eyes were still shut. 'Disgusting and cruel.'

'That's why they always lived so simply. Why they sold their big house and rented a tiny little flat. Rani di was paranoid about not being able to pay for whatever treatment Munni would ultimately need. Even that money is now over. That's why they didn't move here—because living costs are so high in the city.'

'Don't we know it?' Ma muttered, getting up from the sofa.

'Never mind, Ma.' Baba got up too. 'She's got us—we'll manage.'

Mishti and Thamma were left side by side on the sofa.

'What's insurance, Thamma?' Mishti asked, when Thamma didn't say anything.

Thamma took off her glasses. 'It means that you arrange with a company—called an insurance company—that they will help pay your hospital bills. You have to pay them some money every year which they can invest, so that it grows and they can help you when you need it.'

'Do you have insurance, Thamma?'

'Oh yes, we all do. Baba, Ma, me—even you.'

'And what else can have insurance? Pets? Things?'

'Oh, almost anything—cars and houses and all sorts of things in case of accidents and—'

'Then why can't Munni have insurance?'

Thamma screwed up her mouth. 'It's because Munni is what people call disabled—handicapped, retarded, even—'

'But—'

Thamma had started crying again. 'Society is unfair, Mishti. Cruel, unfair, not inclusive—'

Ma had come back with cups of hot tea. She put one in front of Thamma, sat down and took a long sip from her own.

'What's inclusive?'

'It means people who are different in any way— different from most of the other people, what is called the majority—should not be made to feel different. In any way. In the way we see them or treat them or in the way we do things for them.'

Mishti stared at Ma. The corners of her eyes were getting prickly hot again. But Ma didn't notice—she was sipping her tea. Angrily.

'If everything is equal and fair and the same for everybody, why can't Munni get insurance? Tell me that!' Ma banged her empty cup down on the table.

'Aare, Joyeeta, why involve the child in these discussions?' Thamma wiped her nose with her sari. 'What will she do? Poor thing!'

I'm not a poor thing, Mishti wanted to say, but Ma was talking again.

'Why, Ma? Why should she be left out of these discussions? She's old enough to understand unfairness—injustice, inequality, callousness—'

It should have sounded preachy, but in Ma's current mood it didn't. She just looked hot and angry.

'If we are willing to pay a higher premium for Munni because she's at higher risk, who are the insurance companies to say anything?'

'They're the ones who make the rules, Joyeeta,' Thamma said. 'Do we really have a choice? At least, Munni has us to look after her; there are hundreds of others who have no one.'

Mishti remembered what Riya had said. 'But there are places—I know—institu—like hospitals—'

Ma turned her head and Mishti was frightened at the look in her eyes. 'And that would be your solution for Munni? An institution full of strangers?'

'Aah, Joyeeta,' Thamma spoke hurriedly, 'she didn't mean it like that, did you Mishti?'

Mishti could only shake her head.

'See, Mishti,' continued Thamma, signalling to Ma over Mishti's head, 'those places are okay when you have no one, but they don't really look after you properly. Not like your own family, na?'

Her voice was very gentle, but she pressed Mishti's hand with her own. Keep quiet, she was saying, don't argue.

Ma's phone rang just then. 'The hospital!' she pounced on it. 'Hello! Hello! Yes! Yes—oh—'

She looked at Thamma and mouthed, 'She's okay!' before going into her bedroom. Five minutes later, she was back, frowning hard.

'Munni's okay,' she told Thamma. 'No change, but no worse—'

'Then?'

'It was the billing department.'

'Oh!'

'Yes, I must go to the bank. Whatever we paid this morning is already all used up.'

Chapter 8

The days went by and Munni got no better. She was still hooked to the ventilator, which was making her breathe artificially.

'At least, she's getting no worse, Ma,' Baba said after Munni had been in the hospital for almost two weeks.

'Yes, but how long can it go on like this?' Thamma asked. 'How long—'

Mishti knew Thamma was talking about money. Almost immediately after Munni had gone to hospital, the discussion had started. At first, Ma and Baba and Thamma had discussed it only at night, only after Mishti had gone to bed. If they had to bring it up in front of her at all, they talked in hints and signals.

As the days dragged on and everyone stopped smiling and looked worried and harried and grey all the time, nobody really cared any more. Now all the talk was almost always about money. Bills, more bills, expenses, medicines, something called 'consumables'. And the fact that the doctors were feeding Munni through her bloodstream, which was much much more expensive than normal hospital food. Could Munni even taste it, Mishti wondered as the grown-ups discussed it over her head. Sometimes, Mishti thought they even forgot to talk about how Munni was doing.

They were changes at home too. The air conditioner was never switched on now—'it eats electricity, drinks it in great gulps. And anyway, it's not that hot yet.' Mishti looked at the weather app on Ma's phone: it said 40 degrees C.

The next change was Munni's tiffin. It became a regular parade of cheese sandwiches, sometimes interrupted with leftover sabzi rolled up in parathas. No chicken rolls, quiche, bacon puffs or any of the fancy stuff Ma used to make so brilliantly. Riya had taken one sniff at Mishti's tiffin and turned up her nose. 'It's really very annoying—very monotonous—to have you bring the same things over and over again,' she said. 'Look at mine and look at yours!'

Mishti looked at the stale chicken puffs in Riya's box. 'Yours are shop bought,' she said. 'Ma makes mine herself.'

'So why can't she make things like she used to?'

'Because—' started Mishti, then stopped. She didn't really want to discuss Munni with Riya. Or discuss anything more with Riya.

'I'm going,' she said, getting up. 'I'm going to eat what my mother made and you can have what you buy from the shop—'

'We buy because we have the money,' jeered Riya after her, 'and you don't! You don't even have a car!' But Mishti had started running.

'Are we poor, Ma?' she asked Ma that night. It was a question that had been troubling her for some time now. 'Are we very, very poor? Like church mouses? What's a church mouse?'

Ma took a moment to reply; as if she was not really sure of what to say. 'We are—' She cleared her throat. 'Not rich—but very comfortably off. Why do you ask?'

'Because—' Mishti wasn't sure how much to tell Ma, but she needn't have worried.

'Something at school, Mishti?' Ma stretched out a hand.

Mishti clung to Ma, feeling weepy but not wanting to cry. Slowly, a little at a time, she started to tell Ma about all that had happened. How mean Riya had been, how she—and her gang—had laughed and jeered and how Mishti had run away.

'I felt like a coward,' Mishti mumbled against Ma's nice soft belly. 'But I didn't know what to do. I was so angry—so angry—'

'That you could have hit her—' Ma kissed Mishti on the top of her head. 'Never mind, baby, you did the right thing.'

They sat like that for some time. Then, 'Ma?' Mishti lifted her eyes to Ma. 'Are we poor?'

Ma smiled down at her. 'You tell me—what do you think?'

'I don't know.' Mishti shook her head. 'I've never really thought about it—not until—'

'Now—exactly. So doesn't that mean that we're not poor?'

'But—'

'No one has endless money, Mishti. As long as we have enough to eat and a nice house and a comfortable life, why should we worry?'

'And that is also a lot more than a lot of people have—' Baba had entered with Thamma. 'If you know how to manage the money you earn and you have the basic necessities—that's all you need really.'

'When I was a little girl,' said Thamma as she sat down next to Mishti, 'sometimes we didn't have enough to eat. There were eleven of us brothers and sisters and my pishi with her three children and my father was the only person who had a job.'

'What did you do?' Mishti felt very grown-up discussing money matters with everyone.

'Oh, we managed! There were good days and bad days and sometimes we had money only for one meal a day. But no one minded and no one cried. I still remember what fun we always had—all fourteen of us.'

'But Thamma—'

'Love and laughter, Mishti,' Baba said, 'a family—and a house—needs love and laughter, more than they need money.'

'But money helps,' said Thamma, suddenly serious again. 'Here—' she handed Ma a red velvet pouch, the kind Mishti had seen jewellery come out of. 'This is the one—'

Ma turned the pouch bottom up on the bed and something glittery fell out.

'I had saved this for Mishti's wedding.' Thamma held it up sadly. It was a magnificent necklace—gold and diamond and complicated designs dazzling in the overhead light. Mishti hadn't seen it before and she didn't really like any talk of her wedding, but she kept mum.

Suddenly, everyone had become very grim. Almost like crying. And the necklace was really ugly for all its glitter.

'She has to be educated first,' said Baba, getting up, 'then she can buy all the jewellery she wants. There's only so much that can be done on a single income. Come on, Ma—'

He went out with Thamma. Mishti heard them talking again. Snatches of conversation: 'Should last a week', 'the doctors are hopeful'.

'Ma, why don't you have a job?' asked Mishti, suddenly. 'You went to college—' Mishti had seen Ma's graduation picture. 'Wouldn't we have more money if you worked?'

Ma laughed, a small sad whisper of a laugh. 'I wish I could, Mishti, I really do. Apart from the money, it's just such a waste of a brain. I did work till right before we had you. And even for a couple of years after you were born. You wouldn't remember, but when you were about three years old, Thamma had a bad fall—'

'That's why she walks so slowly!'

'Yes, she broke her hip, poor thing, and the arthritis in her hands was getting very bad, so she really couldn't look after a frisky toddler any more. And Didums—'

'Is with Sunu mama.'

Didums was Ma's mother. She lived in America with Sunu mama—Ma's brother—and his family and only ever visited every two or three years. For some reason, Mishti got the feeling that Didums didn't really like Thamma or Baba, but no one ever talked about that or said anything.

'Anyway, I didn't want to leave you with an outsider, so we didn't get an ayah or anything. We managed fine, Mishti.'

'But—' the words stuck in Mishti's throat. 'I'm— I'm sorry—'

'Don't be.' Ma stroked her hair so lovingly the tears sprang to her eyes again. 'I don't have any regrets at all—it's fine; really and truly it is. Once you grow up a little and can do more things for yourself, perhaps I *will* go back to work—we'll see. And anyway, it's never been a problem before.'

Not till Munni came, said Mishti to herself, but not angrily. She wasn't angry with Munni any more and that surprised her when she thought about it, but not very much. The grown-ups were too troubled to bother with her, but they would have been quite astonished to know that she was just as worried about Munni as they were.

'How long will the necklace last, Ma?' she whispered next morning.

'Not very long,' Ma whispered back. 'But fingers crossed—all we can do is hope and pray.'

Two days later, the precious necklace was sold and Mishti felt she had turned into a stopwatch. Or the timer on Ma's oven. As if they only had so much time and then everything would suddenly stop. Like the last over of a cricket match or the final lap of a race. As if she was holding her breath, waiting—waiting—for something to happen. All she wanted to do was to crawl into a hole and go to sleep and then wake up to find Munni home again.

Nobody spoke about Munni any more. They came and went like robots, going to the hospital because they had to; doing everything that needed to be done, but Mishti could see that their hearts were not really in it. Ma and Baba went about looking pinched and grey and permanently exhausted. But it was Thamma who really scared Mishti, when one day—just like that—she stopped using her favourite Chanel No. 5.

Munni had now been in hospital for a month. Somedays, Mishti thought Munni would never get better—did that mean she was going to die? Mishti had never seen anyone dying. Both her grandfathers had died well before she was born and she had only ever seen them in photographs. Thamma had her illnesses on and off, but she always got better. If Munni died—but she didn't want to think of that just yet, there was something else she had to know.

'Thamma, has your No. 5 finished?'

Thamma wiped her eyes. For the last week or so, Thamma had been crying nearly all the time.

But even so, she had never left off using the perfume. Mishti was seriously scared; she had never—ever—seen Thamma without her smell.

'No, Mishti, I just don't want to use it any more.'

'Why, Thamma?'

'I just don't feel like it, Mishti. I just—'

'But why? Is it to save money?'

'Mishti,' Ma cut in. 'Don't be rude.'

'She's not being rude, Joyi, she's asking a valid question,' Baba said. 'No Mishti, it's not about money—not this time, at least—'

'Then?'

But Thamma just pressed trembling fingers to her mouth. Baba put his arms around her quickly. 'Ma, it's all right,' he said and then spoke to Mishti, 'Dadu—my father—gave Thamma her first bottle of Chanel No. 5

when they were married. In those days, about sixty years ago, foreign perfumes were very rare in India. Dadu had brought it back from Paris and when it became Thamma's favourite, he made sure he gave her a bottle every year.'

'I have never used anything else,' said Thamma. 'Even when your Dadu died, it reminded me of him, of all the happy times we had together, the memories . . .'

No one said anything for some time. Thamma started to speak, but Baba's phone shrilled out just then.

'The hospital!' He jumped up and rushed into the bedroom. Mishti only heard some excited chattering before Baba shut the door.

'What were you saying, Ma?' said Ma loudly. On purpose, Mishti knew, otherwise they would all be trying to listen to the conversation.

'About the perfume,' Mishti added helpfully. 'Na, Thamma?'

'Only a drop,' said Thamma in a flat voice, 'and it would make me so happy. Now . . . now . . . there is nothing happy or hopeful any more. It seems you'll get your wish, after all, Mishti.'

What wish? thought Mishti, but Baba had come back, looking very strange. Excited, not really happy, but not sad either. Like a bubbling pot.

'She's better,' he blurted out, 'not a lot—just a little— but finally everything seems to be going in the right direction. After all these weeks!' He stopped and looked around. 'They want—they want—they said—'

'Sit down,' said Ma. 'Sit down and calm down.'

'Take a deep breath, Baba,' said Mishti suddenly; why she didn't know. It just came out on its own.

Baba did both. He stopped moving, took a deep breath, then dropped down next to Thamma on the sofa.

What he explained was both scary and exciting. After all those weeks on the ventilator, Munni had suddenly decided to get better. Or at least, she had started getting better—a little at a time. Now the doctors wanted to see how much she could do on her own, by taking away—very, very carefully—her drips and machines and medicines. One by one—very, very slowly—to see how she responded to those changes.

'They said it would take some time—anything from a week to two, maybe more—and—'

'Will the necklace last till then?' Mishti interrupted; she had to know.

'We'll make sure it does,' said Ma. 'If Munni is putting up a fight, we must do all we can to help—'

'Only—' Baba said, then stopped uncertainly and looked at Ma.

'Well?' Thamma lifted her head.

Baba licked his lips and looked down at his hands. 'They said—the doctors said—' he continued in a whisper, 'after the last month, it would be a miracle if Munni does survive. At the moment, they are just barely keeping her alive. But if she hadn't shown signs of improvement, they would have asked us how long we would have liked to continue with her treatment. Not just in terms of money but also because there would be no point—'

'So what are they saying now?' Ma asked.

'That after what they call a reasonable trial, they have to stop. And that we must be prepared—'

'To let her go.' Thamma stood up. 'I have known this for some time, Rajat, and I am prepared. Miracles don't happen.' She walked away with slow tired steps.

Baba got up as well. He looked at Ma again, shrugged and went after Thamma. Mishti and Ma were left sitting on the sofa, Ma staring at the TV with a frown.

But Mishti wanted things explained clearly.

'What is a reasonable trial, Ma?'

'It means,' Ma was frowning fiercely at the TV, 'that sometimes, even after weeks and weeks of good treatment, patients can't breathe—or stay alive— on their own. It means,' she swallowed, 'that once everything that could be *reasonably* done has been done—and tried—treatment may still not work. Even the best treatment—'

'So what do they do?' Mishti didn't like where this conversation was going, but she couldn't stop herself.

87

'They—' Ma's eyes were brimming over, 'they—stop treatment—they—'

'They let her die?' Mishti started crying. 'They let her die? They kill her? How can they just kill her?'

She clung to her mother, crying loudly. Ma was crying too, but she put her arms around Mishti and held her tight. But there was one last question Mishti had to ask. Something had suddenly clicked into place while Baba had been talking.

'Ma,' she whispered through her tears, 'is this all happening because of my wish? You know when I said I wished she was dead? Is it, Ma?'

Mishti was shaking with fear. Could you actually ill-wish someone so hard that they would die? And after suffering like this? Did that mean anyone could ill-wish anyone else? Could anyone ill-wish her? Or Ma? Baba? Thamma? Anyone who didn't like them? Riya, for example? Now that they weren't friends any more? She tugged at Ma's T-shirt with sweaty fingers. 'Ma-Ma—'

'No, you silly girl.' Ma almost laughed through her tears. 'It doesn't work like that. How can it? Don't be silly! How can you wish someone dead? Just like that? Then people would drop dead all the time—right, left and centre!'

'But I said—'

'I know what you said,' Ma wiped Mishti's cheeks, 'and it wasn't a nice thing to say. But you were upset and angry and—and you don't feel like that now, do you?'

88

Mishti shook her head hard—she felt very differently; had felt very differently for a very long time now. 'I don't want Munni to die—'

'None of us do.' Ma got up. 'Try good-wishing for a change. Try wishing her well-well-well. Now, come on, let's eat.'

'But, Ma,' Mishti was still worried, 'when will we know what's happening? If I'm in school, how will I know?'

Mishti refused to go to school the next day. And the next. And the next. And the whole week—'not till I know what's going to happen!'

Also, she had a plan. A secret plan that had popped into her head after Ma's talk of good-wishing. And she wanted to carry it out without any disruption. The 'Munni Bachao' plan, Riya would have called it.

'I wish Munni gets well and comes home.' That was the only wish she had at the moment. Over and over and over, she repeated it in her head, sometimes whispering it fiercely aloud when she was alone. Surely, if she could say it all the time—every day—for as long as she was awake, it would take away the effects of her horrible ill-wish?

A week went by. Ten days. Fifteen days of the 'reasonable trial'. And slowly, but surely, it seemed that the 'Munni Bachao' plan was working. Another necklace had to be sold—this time Ma's. But every day, Munni got better, a little at a time, but definitely better than the day before.

One by one, the machines came off. After more than two months, she started breathing on her own. A few days later, the feeding line in her neck was removed. Till, at last, she was on one single drip.

Then, one day, Baba came rushing home crying like a baby.

'She sat up and smiled and called me baba!' he yelled. 'She's eating on her own—they're going to move her out of intensive care—she's going to come home!'

One unbelieving stunned moment later, everyone sprang to their feet. And shouted and cried and hugged each other all at once. Everyone wanted to talk and no one wanted to listen—they had all gone mad. Laughing, crying, hiccupping with joy. Till—suddenly, unbelievably—Ma put on some loud jangly music and they danced and danced till they could dance no longer. Even Thamma.

'Let's celebrate,' said Thamma, after she had recovered her breath, 'let's order some pizza for dinner!'

'No, not today!' Mishti said automatically. 'Not now—when Munni comes home. She likes pizza.'

And after more than two dark, terrible months, it seemed that Munni Monster was going to come home after all.

The day after the crazy dance party, the doctors moved Munni out of the intensive care department, but Mishti still refused to go to school. 'After Munni comes home,' she said every time someone mentioned it. She was wishing harder than ever. One part of her good-wishing had come true; surely, surely, *surely*, the other would too?

On the day Munni was supposed to be discharged from hospital, Mishti was ready before anyone else. All night she had tossed and turned and worried herself almost to the point of a headache. Would Munni really come home? Or was it all a dream? A nightmare? In which everything goes wrong at the last minute?

The grown-ups were also fretting. The ride to the hospital didn't help. Thamma had insisted on coming along, so it was a tight squash inside the taxi, but no one noticed. They were all thinking about Munni.

Through the hospital entrance, hopping from one foot to the other, while Ma argued with the taxi driver. Then up, up, up four floors in a lift that smelt of unwashed people and disinfectant and *hospital*. Then through a long, long never-ending grey corridor, Ma dragging her by the hand, all the while saying 'Please, please, please, *please*', to herself. Till, at last, they had opened the doors with a screech and stepped inside Munni's ward.

'Open your eyes, Mishti,' Ma said suddenly. 'Look—there's Munni!'

Mishti looked.

And could contain herself no longer. Throwing off Ma's hand, she rushed across the ward, ignoring

91

Thamma's 'Wait, Mishti!', dodging the trolleys and beds and bits of equipment, winding her way through the patients and nurses and doctors till, at last, she came to a stop at the foot of Munni's bed.

Even that was only for one panting moment. Ignoring all the people who were rushing to see what had happened, she shoved the table aside and threw herself weeping at Munni's lunch-smeared dress.

And, as if nothing at all had happened between then and now in the terrifying weeks that they had been apart, Munni crowed with delight. Over Ma's delighted laughter, Baba's cheers, Thamma's sobs and spontaneous applause from the whole ward, rose the well-loved cackle she had never thought to hear again: 'Mit-ti! Mit-ti! Mɪᴛ-ᴛɪ!'

Afterword

Up until I got married and came to live with my husband's family (nearly two decades ago now!), I had never lived with anyone quite like Munni Monster. As doctors, we have to talk to and look after many different types of people, but living with them, as Mishti's mother tells her, is an entirely different proposition.

The character of Munni is based on an aunt-by-marriage, wonderfully joyous and fiercely independent. Fiercely independent in spirit, much like Munni, for all that she has to depend on others for her physical needs. With firm likes, dislikes and opinions, especially about food! A lot of who she is and how she lives life has gone into the making of Munni. As well as the problems that are uniquely her own, different from us so-called 'normal' people.

About three out of every one thousand children born in India have cerebral palsy[1]. That's a lot of children when you think about statistics and numbers. Twenty-five million children are born in India every year[2], which is one out of five childbirths worldwide. Even with a child dying every minute, there are about 250 million children in the Indian school system at any given time[3].

Now, more than previously, there are many organizations doing sterling work for people with special needs, both children and older people. Like Munni, the grandmother who crawls, more and more children born with cerebral palsy are surviving into adulthood, middle age and even old age. A major reason for this is that healthcare has improved and there is a lot more awareness around these 'special' people.

The trouble is, there isn't just one thing 'wrong' with children born with cerebral palsy. They have problems with walking, talking, eating, speaking—you name it, they seem to have it. And about one-third to half of them find it difficult to understand and process the world around them. In medical jargon, this is called 'cognitive impairment', you may have heard it referred to as 'mental retardation'. Nowadays, much more sensibly, it's just called 'learning disabilities'. Because a lot of these people are not too great with words, it becomes even more difficult to understand the level of their disability. Like Munni, who had a lot to say—a lot of things that made perfect sense—but couldn't, because she couldn't find the words. Think of being in a country where you can't make yourself understood simply because you don't know their language and they don't understand yours.

What makes it even more complicated, is that no one has exactly the same set of symptoms as the next. If you stood all the Munnis in a line, you would be hard pressed to find two who were a perfect match. And the level of disabilities is never uniform. Some have very mild symptoms, others are so severely affected that they may not walk or talk at all, just lie on a bed all their lives and need everything done for them.

For those who want to know more, there is a lot of information out there, but it always makes sense to verify your sources. A good place to start is the Indian Institute of Cerebral Palsy (IICP) website (www.iicpindia.org) or the Special Olympics website (www.specialolympics.org).

For more information, especially in the Indian context, there is a list overleaf.

References

1. Chauhan, Anil, et al. 'Prevalence of Cerebral Palsy in Indian Children: A Systematic Review and Meta-Analysis'. *Indian Journal of Pediatrics.* 2019. Epub 2019 Jul 13.

2. 'Newborn and Child Health'. UNICEF. Retrieved from https://www.unicef.org/india/what-we-do/newborn-and-child-health

3. 'Catalysing Transformational Change in School Education'. UNICEF. Retrieved from https://www.unicef.org/india/reports/catalysing-transformational-change-school-education

List of Organizations Working with Cerebral Palsy

(A very big thank you to Dr Sudha Kaul, Founder, Indian Institute of Cerebral Palsy for this list.)

1. Vidya Sagar: vidyasagar.co.in
2. Action for Ability Development and Inclusion: aadi-india.org
3. ADAPT (formerly known as Spastics Society of India)
4. Spastics Society of Karnataka: spasticssocietyofkarnataka.org
5. Shishu Sarothi: www.shishusarothi.org
6. KIRAN Village: kiranvillage.org
7. The Spastics Society of Tamil Nadu (SPASTN)
8. Indian Academy of Cerebral Palsy (IACP): iacp.co.in
9. Ambika Sishu Kendra: ambikasishukendra.org
10. ICD Centre for Treament for Children with Cerebral Palsy: www.icddelhi.org
11. Prerona Pratibandhi Sishu Bikash Kendra: preronaorg.webs.com/
12. Deepshikha Institute for Child Development and Mental Health: deepshikhaindia.org
13. Raksha Society: www.facebook.com/RakshaSociety
14. Dwar Jingkyrmen School for Children in Need: megscpwd.gov.in/dwarjingkyrmen/about-us
15. Spastic Society of Mizoram: www.facebook.com/SpasticSocietyMizoram
16. Open Learning Systems—Championing Child Rights: olsbbsr.or
17. Jalpaiguri Welfare Organization: jalpaguriwelfare.org

Madhurima Vidyarthi is an endocrinologist who always wanted to be a writer. She trained in London for many years and then returned to live and work in Calcutta.

Munni Monster is her second book, but she is planning to write many more.

When she is not writing—books or prescriptions—Madhurima likes to travel, eat good food and delve into history. She lives in an untidy house full of unruly members and desperately wants a dog.

Find out more about her at www.madhurimavidyarthi.com

Instagram - https://www.instagram.com/madhurimavidyarthi/

Tanvi Bhat is a children's book illustrator and author who has created books for publishers like Pratham Books, Duckbill and Tulika Books, to name a few. She likes working with watercolours and gouache when making pictures, and scribbling on scraps of paper that she's constantly losing when she writes.